PIRATE CAMPOUT

BASED ON THE EPISODE WRITTEN BY MARK DROP

ADAPTED BY BILL SCOLLON

ILLUSTRATED BY CHARACTER BUILDING STUDIO

AND THE DISNEY STORYBOOK ART TEAM

DISNEY PRESS

New York • Los Angeles

"Rise and shine," says Skully.
"It's pirate campout day!"
Jake and his crew will camp
near Doubloon Lagoon.

The crew sets sail for Shipwreck Beach.
"We're off, mateys!" calls Jake.

“Let’s hike to Doubloon Lagoon!”
says Jake.
“A lagoon of Gold Doubloons!”
says Hook. “I must have it!”

Hook catches up to Jake.
"We want to come, too," he says.
"Join us," Jake says.
"We can camp together!"

Oops! Hook gets rolled up in his tent.

"Help!" he calls.

Cubby uses his map.
He leads them to Campout Clearing.
"Way to go," says Izzy.
"We can set up our tents here."

Goldfish!

Hook falls onto Jake's tent.
It rips apart.
"Oh, my," says Smee.
"Both tents are a mess!"

"Where will we sleep?" asks Cubby.
"I have an idea," Izzy says.
"We can make one big tent!"

Izzy finds big leaves.
Jake finds bamboo poles.
Cubby uses parts of the tents.

"It is time for a spooky story,"
says Jake.
"I call it 'The Monster of
Doubloon Lagoon'!"

“Pirates came to Doubloon Lagoon.
They were looking for gold.

But something spooky was
in the water.
It banged into their boat!"

What are pirates
afraid of?

“What was it?” asks Bones.

“It was a monster,” says Jake.

“With eight legs and eight hooks!”

“Ahhh!” the pirates scream.

Hook's crew climbs up a tree.
"Come down," says Jake.
"It is only a story!"

The daaaark!

The next day, Cubby leads the way.
Doubloon Lagoon is ahead.

"Don't turn here," says Cubby.
"That's Snail Slime Trail!"

Hook does not listen.
He slides down Snail Slime Trail.
Whoosh! Hook flies into the air!

Hook runs to Doubloon Lagoon.
"All that gold is mine!" he calls.

Splash!
Hook falls into the lagoon.

Hook wants to be first to
Doubloon Lagoon.
He traps Jake and his crew
under a net!

Jake cuts the net.
"Come on, mateys," he says.
"We have to save Hook!"

Cubby finds the lagoon.
It looks just like a Doubloon!
"Way to go, Cubby!" says Jake.

“The monster!” calls Hook.
“It is trying to get me.”
“That is not a monster,” says Jake.
“The octopus is our friend.”

How many arms does the octopus have?

Izzy uses her Pixie Dust.

The crew pulls Hook out of the lagoon!

"Bah!" says Hook. "There is no gold here.
Back to the ship, men."

"Bye-bye, sea pups," says Smee.

Jake and his crew camp out at home.
"I want to tell a story," Cubby says.
"'The Tale of the Spooky Coconut.'"
"Yo-ho! Way to go, Cubby!" says Jake.

Ahoy, mateys! Do you want to join my pirate crew? Then just say the pirate password: "Yo-ho-ho!" As part of my crew, you'll need to learn the Never Land pirate pledge.

DISNEY PRESS

First Edition 10 9 8 7 6 5 4 3 2
ISBN 978-1-4231-8398-3

G658-7729-4-14166

Manufactured in the USA
For more Disney Press fun, visit www.disneybooks.com

SUSTAINABLE FORESTRY INITIATIVE
Certified Chain of Custody
Promoting Sustainable Forestry
www.sfiprogram.org
SFI-01415
The SFI label applies to the text stock